DEDICATION:
We dedicate this book to the people of South Africa and the preservation of African wildlife, and to the MalaMala Game Reserve, where the thrill of adventure sowed the seeds for this book.

Nicole
&
Rachael,
Travel to the
South African bush.
Learn about animals
with Riley. Watch out for
the grumpy elephant!
Best Wishes,

Amanda

Reading takes you places.

SAFARI IN SOUTH AFRICA

ADVENTURES OF RILEY

BY AMANDA LUMRY
& LAURA HURWITZ

ILLUSTRATED BY
SARAH MCINTYRE

EaglemonT
Press

All photographs by Amanda Lumry except:
cover inset vulture/wild dog © Adrian Bailey/Aurora
cover inset black rhino, pg. 8 wild dogs and pg. 18
South African galago © Paul Funston
pg. 27 black rhino © Gerald Hinde

Illustrations ©2003 by Sarah McIntyre
Editing and Finished Layouts by Michael E. Penman

Digital Imaging by Embassy Graphics, Canada
Printed in China by Midas Printing International Limited

Library of Congress Control Number: 2003105372

ISBN: 0-9662257-8-3

A portion of the proceeds from your purchase
of this licensed product supports the stated educational
mission of the Smithsonian Institution -"the increase
and diffusion of knowledge." The name of the
Smithsonian Institution and the sunburst logo are registered
trademarks of the Smithsonian Institution and are registered in
the U.S. Patent and Trademark Office.
www.si.edu

2% of the proceeds from this book will be
donated to the Wildlife Conservation Society.
http://wcs.org

A royalty of approximately 1% of
the estimated retail price of this
book will be received by World
Wildlife Fund (WWF). The Panda Device
and WWF are registered trademarks. All rights
reserved by World Wildlife Fund, Inc.
www.worldwildlife.org

A special thank you
to all the scientists
who collaborated
on this project.
Your time and
assistance is very
much appreciated.

EaglemonT
Press

First edition published 2003
by Eaglemont Press
PMB 741
15600 NE 8th #B-1
Bellevue, WA 98008
(425) 462-6618
info@eaglemontpress.com
www.eaglemontpress.com

Dear Riley,

Greetings from your wild Uncle Max!
We are off again on another adventure! I'm
so happy that you could join me, your Aunt
Martha, and your Cousin Alice on safari in
the South African bush.

We are going to give the animal
population a "check up." We won't actually
be taking their temperatures or giving them
shots, but we will be counting the members
of their families, especially babies, to see if
their numbers are increasing or decreasing.
Your parents tell me that you are
good at arithmetic, so this should be a snap!

Cheers,

Uncle Max

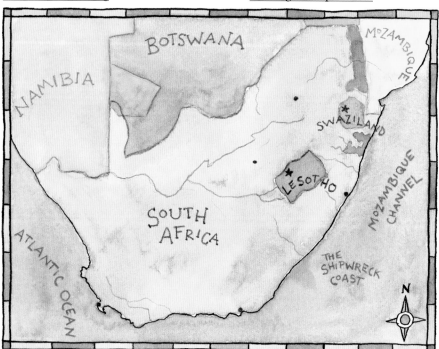

"You're finally here!" Alice squealed, almost knocking Riley over with a bear hug.

Aunt Martha smiled, "Welcome to Johannesburg!"

"You'll barely have a chance to put your feet on the ground, Carrot Top. We have one more short flight to camp. Are you game? Sorry, bad joke," winked Uncle Max.

1

The small plane flew them far away from the city and deep into the African bush. Once they landed, two men greeted them.

"Hello, my name is Chad," said the first man. "I will be your guide, or ranger, as we are known here."

"And my name is Hendrik," said the other man. "I will be your tracker," he said, shaking Riley's hand. They headed off towards camp.

"Tracker? What's a tracker?" asked Alice.

"I watch for animals and birds, then point them out for everyone to see," said Hendrik. "Sitting up here in the vehicle helps me find them. Look! There is a lilac-breasted roller."

LILAC-BREASTED ROLLER

➤ They get their name from their funny, floppy way of flying.

➤ They chase and eat insects around other animals' feet.

➤ They follow fires to look for insects that have been scared away.

Dr. Neil Burgess
Senior Conservation Scientist

World Wildlife Fund

3

After unpacking, they ate lunch on the deck. Alice and Riley could hardly sit still.

WHEN ON SAFARI

➤ No standing up in the vehicle. This can cause the animals to run away or want to eat you!

➤ Shhh... If you want to see the animals up close, you have to be as quiet as a mouse.

"We're ready to start our game drive whenever you are," said Chad.

As they were loading their gear into the car, Uncle Max suddenly turned around and ran off. He quickly returned out of breath. "I almost forgot my GPS unit. That's where I keep track of everything we see."

Uncle Max spoke into his tape recorder. "Testing. One...two...three! This is Professor Maxwell. I am here in South Africa with my ace counting team. It is day one and we are ready to go!"

NYALA

➤ Males' fur changes from a reddish brown to a brown-gray with age.

➤ Fighting between male nyala is occasionally to the death.

➤ They stand on their hind legs in order to reach higher branches to feed.

Dr. Robert S. Hoffmann
Senior
Scientist

Smithsonian
Institution

They had not gone far when Hendrik saw some antelope. "These nyala are only found in southern Africa."

As Uncle Max was busy entering their first sighting into his GPS, the antelope looked up in alarm and leapt into the bush.

"Why did they leave? Did we scare them?" asked Riley.

"No, I think there might be danger close by," Chad said.

"Ohh!" whispered Riley and Alice.

At least I got a great picture before they ran away, Riley thought to himself.

6

Not far from the nyala, they came across two lively cheetah cubs.

"They seem to be playing soccer, cheetah style," said Aunt Martha.

"Yeah! A stinky game, considering their ball is made of elephant poop!" said Chad.

"Yuck!" said Alice.

"I bet it was the cheetahs that scared the nyala," said Riley.

"Quite likely," answered Uncle Max, "since the nyala need to protect their young from predators, including cheetahs."

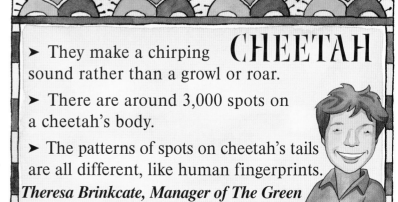

CHEETAH

➤ They make a chirping sound rather than a growl or roar.

➤ There are around 3,000 spots on a cheetah's body.

➤ The patterns of spots on cheetah's tails are all different, like human fingerprints.

Theresa Brinkcate, Manager of The Green Trust South Africa, World Wildlife Fund

On the way back to camp, Hendrik signaled Chad to stop the vehicle. There was a pack of small animals hiding in the grass.

"Look! Dogs!" said Alice.

"Yes, those are dogs, but not the kind you would have as pets. Those are African wild dogs with their pups," said Hendrik.

"What a rare treat!" said Uncle Max, happily.

"You see, wild dogs are becoming harder to find in South Africa as people take over the land the dogs call home."

➤ They live in groups called packs, which have two to thirty members.

➤ The adults feed their young with food they eat first and then spit out. Yuck!

➤ They are endangered because people see them as pests and hunt them.

WILD DOG

Dr. Joshua Ginsberg
Director, Asia
Regional Program
Wildlife Conservation Society

That night everyone yawned their way through dinner and went straight to bed.

"We sure saw a lot of babies today," said Riley, sleepily.

"Yes, we did," said Uncle Max. "I was happy to see the nyala as well as the wild dogs and cheetahs. In nature, there needs to be a balance between prey and predator. Without a balance, neither one can survive..."

He looked over and saw that Riley had fallen fast asleep.

They started the next morning with another game drive.
"Can I sit in the back with you today, Hendrik?" asked Riley.
"Of course," said Hendrik.

Passing through a wooded area, Alice saw
something fly over her head.

10

"Look!" she cried, pointing. "Monkeys! In Nepal a monkey stole my Dad's underwear. Remember that, Riley?"

"I sure do!" he replied.

"Huh? How interesting," said Chad, giving them both a funny look. "These are actually baboons, and as far as I know, *baboons* don't wear any clothes."

The leaping baboons were tricky to count! Uncle Max finally finished and they moved on.

BABOON
➤ Baboons live in groups of 50 to 200.
➤ They are omnivores, which mean they eat both plants and animals.
➤ They sleep in trees to stay safe from hyenas, lions and other predators.

Dr. Richard W. Thorington, Jr.
Curator of Mammals
Smithsonian Institution

➤ Mother giraffes stand up while giving birth so they can look for predators.

➤ Baby giraffes can stand up within fifteen minutes after they are born.

➤ They can grow up to 18ft/5.5m high and are the tallest animals in the world.

Jennifer D'Amico Hales

Senior Conservation Specialist

World Wildlife Fund

GIRAFFE

Hendrik motioned to them. "Shh... Up ahead is a mother giraffe with her baby."

Watching the giraffes munch made Riley hungry. He pulled out a chocolate bar and wolfed it down, dropping the wrapper to the ground. He thought nothing of it as they headed towards the river.

On the other side of some tall reeds, a herd of elephants stood drinking.

"Look! Three babies," counte Alice. "They are sooo sweet!"

A mother elephant flapped her ears and stomped towards them.

"Time to go!" said Chad. "Female elephants are very protective of their young."

"It would not take much for that elephant to push this car over," Uncle Max said nervously as they drove away.

ELEPHANT

➤ Elephants are usually led by a wise old female elephant.

➤ They enjoy spending time together, especially near water.

➤ Adult elephants are too big for predators, such as lions, to bring down.

Dr. Rob Little
Conservation Director
World Wildlife Fund
South Africa

Just then, the back tire sank into the soft mud. They were stuck and the elephant was still hot on their trail! "Riley, please hold this!" said Uncle Max, handing him his tape recorder. He jumped out to help the other adults. Riley and Alice held their breath as the elephant charged closer. The earth shook with each step.

Squirming in his seat, Riley dropped the tape recorder. A thunderous lion's roar echoed up and down the river. The adults froze at the sound, while the elephant turned and crashed into the reeds.

With no danger in sight, all eyes turned to a bright red Riley.

"Sorry," he said, "I dropped the tape recorder when I got scared."

ROAR

"Good thing you did," Uncle Max grinned. "It seems the old lion noises I taped in the Serengeti sure scared that elephant. Good job, Carrot Top!"

BLACK AND WHITE RHINO DIFFERENCES
➤ White rhinos get their name from their wide lips. The Afrikaans word for wide sounds like "white."
➤ Black rhinos are usually darker than white rhinos and have hooked upper lips.

Eric Dinerstein, Chief Scientist, Vice President for Science, World Wildlife Fund

Soon they were all out of the mud *and hopefully out of danger!*

"Look over behind that bush!" whispered Riley. "I thought it was that grumpy elephant again, but it is a black rhino instead."

"Good sighting!" Hendrik said. "You're close, but this is really a WHITE rhino and her baby. BLACK rhinos are endangered and really hard to find because they have been poached."

"Poached? Like an egg?" asked Alice.

"Not exactly," said Uncle Max. "Poaching is when an animal is illegally hunted and killed for its skin or horns, which are sold for a lot of money. Entire species have been killed off, and the black rhino could be next."

"That is so sad," Riley said.

After the sun set, they started bac to camp. Hendrik whistled to Chad to slow down and aimed his spotlight at a little furry creature.

"Here we have a South African galago, also known as a bushbaby!" said Hendrik.

"I read about those in school," Riley said. "They pee on their hands and feet to help them grip tree branche when they jump and climb."

"I hope that doesn't give you any ideas!" Uncle Max chuckled.

SOUTH AFRICAN GALAGO

➤ They have big eyes to help them see at night.

➤ They eat both plants and animals, but their favorite food is GRASSHOPPERS!

Dr. Colleen McCann
Curator of Primates
Wildlife Conservation Society

18

Under the stars they
ate dinner in a boma,
which is a roofless hut
made of tall reeds.
Riley and Alice danced
and sang with the women
who worked at the camp.

19

After a good night's sleep, they drove to the top of a kopje to watch the sunrise.

For breakfast, they nibbled on muffins while sipping tea and hot cocoa.

20

The car's engine began to sputter on their way down the kopje.

"I bet the radiator needs water again," said Chad.

"Let's get some from the river," suggested Hendrik.

"Can I help?" begged Riley. Hendrik nodded. Together they knelt down to fill a bottle. A mother hippo and her baby popped out of the water. The mother made a loud honking sound.

"Let's leave while we still can," said Hendrik. "I think we woke them up and they sure sound grouchy!"

HIPPOPOTAMUS

➤ Hippos kill more humans than any other African animal. When surprised, they may bite or squash their victim to reach their water hole.

➤ They are herbivores. No meat for them!

➤ They spend most of the day in the water so they don't get sunburned!

Dr. Jesus E. Maldonado
Research Geneticist
Smithsonian
Institution

21

With water in the radiator, the vehicle ran much better. They didn't get very far because they soon met a roadblock of Cape buffalo. Riley and Alice counted ten babies. The air around them was full of bugs, swishing tails, and busy birds known as oxpeckers. Uncle Max reached into his bag to pull out his GPS, but was shocked to find it wasn't there!

CAPE BUFFALO

➤ The males' horns grow together to form a helmet.

➤ They weigh between 900 and 2,000 lbs (408 and 907 kg).

➤ They roam and graze in large herds.

Dr. Pat Thomas
Curator of Mammalogy
Wildlife Conservation Society

Oxpeckers help Cape buffalo by eating ticks, bugs, ear wax and cleaning their open wounds.

Back at camp, everyone helped Uncle Max look for his GPS, but they had no success. He was very upset, so they decided to take his mind off of it by going for a swim.

Chad smiled. "On such a hot day, you'd better be on the lookout for any wild animals that might want to cool off with you in the pool!"

23

On the afternoon game drive, Alice asked, "Are those baby leopards?"

"Great spotting, Alice!" laughed Uncle Max, poking Riley in the ribs.

One leopard started choking and coughed up a bright red object.

"It's a wrapper!" Hendrik said, picking it up with a long stick.

"I dropped that yesterday! I didn't know something so small could hurt an animal," Riley said.

"Litter of any size or amount can cause a big problem. We all share this world and we have to look   out for animals," said Hendrik. Riley nodded, taking it all in.

LEOPARD

➤ They are good at climbing trees–unlike lions and cheetahs.

➤ They hide their food in tree branches so predators and scavengers can't steal it.

➤ They hardly make any sound except a small cough to tell other animals to stay away.

Lisa Padfield, Deputy Director of Conservation, World Wildlife Fund–South Africa

24

Further down the road, Hendrik pointed at three napping lionesses and their chubby cubs, which rolled playfully around them.

"I count six lion cubs, all healthy," said Uncle Max into his tape recorder. "A sighting like this is just what I hoped for. Seeing all of these animals tells me that their population is growing at a good rate."

LION

➤ Lionesses live together in prides with their young.

➤ Lionesses frequently do the food hunting, but the lions eat first, lionesses next and the young eat last.

Dr. Graeme Patterson, Assistant Director
Africa Regional Program, Wildlife
Conservation
Society

He sighed, "If only I could find my GPS unit and record this sighting properly."

"Don't worry, Uncle Max!" said Riley. "I wrote everything down for you. See?"

eopards II

25

Hendrik whistled quietly. "I don't believe my eyes."

"Is that what I think it is?" asked Chad.

"Yes," said Hendrik. "A black rhino! We have not seen one here in years."

"It has a wound on its side, probably caused by a poacher's bullet," Uncle Max said, shaking his head. "This rhino was lucky to have gotten away."

Chad radioed the news back to the camp.

As they were leaving, Riley nudged Alice, "Look at that! I only dropped a little wrapper, but that piece of litter is so big a lion could choke on it."

Uncle Max whooped, "Riley! That's my GPS! It must have fallen out last night when we were on our way back to camp!"

► They are hunted because their horns are wanted for traditional Asian medicine.

► Black rhinos pee and poop on trails to let other rhinos know where they are and where they've been.

Dr. George Amato
Director
Science Resource Center
Wildlife Conservation Society

BLACK RHINO

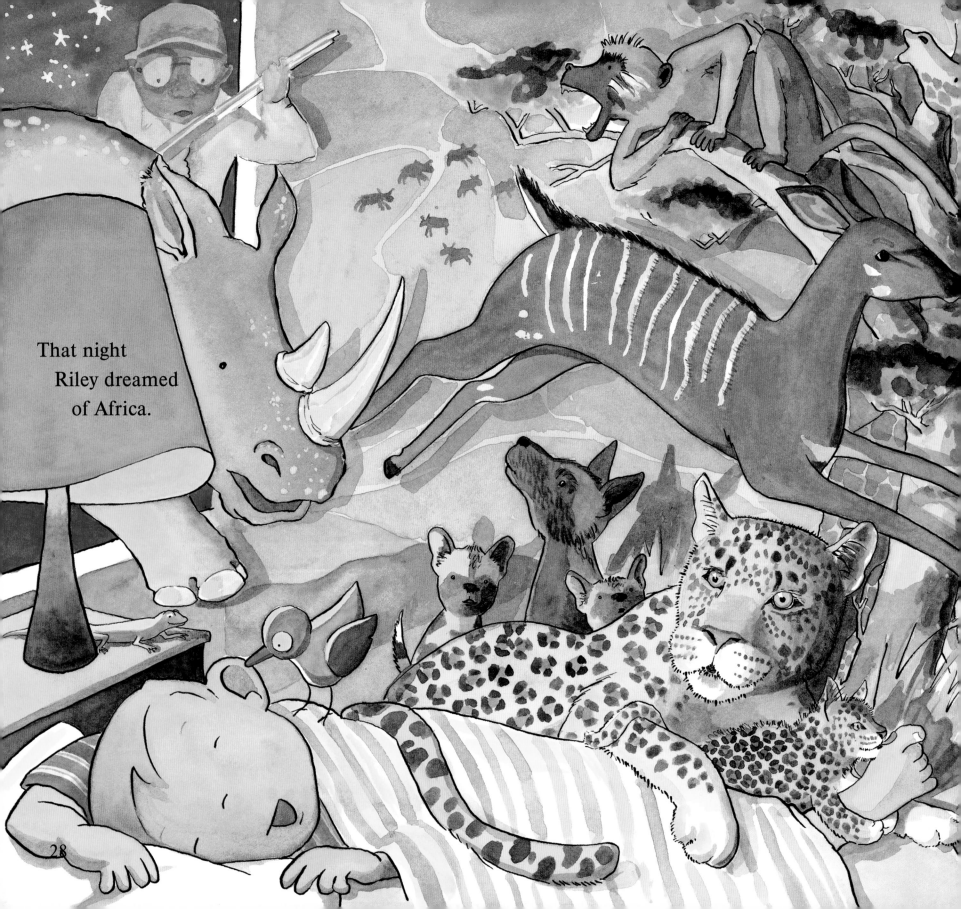

That night
Riley dreamed
of Africa.

28

"Good morning!" beamed Uncle Max. "I am so glad that you found my GPS, Carrot Top. You saved the day, and maybe some animals as well. The animal population here is strong, but poaching is still a big problem," he said, speedily typing away.

He finally looked up, "Let's go eat! I'm as hungry as a lion!"

At the table, Chad said, "I thought you would like to know we received a report. The black rhino was spotted heading into Mozambique."

"I wish we could follow it," Alice said.

"These journeys are a lot easier for animals, since they don't have to make travel plans and get passports," said Uncle Max. "It is up to the governments to allow them to move freely so they can find food and other herds."

They headed to the airstrip. "Thanks for letting me sit with you!" Riley said, giving Hendrik a hug. "I wish I could be a tracker when I grow up."

"You would make a fine one!" Hendrik told him, handing him a brimmed hat just like his. "This is for you, so you can practice your tracking skills."

TRACKER RILEY
- ➤ Your local animal expert needs lots of chocolate for energy!
- ➤ Careful! Litter can harm your pets.
- ➤ Cats like to lay in the sun, but can get angry if you bother them!

Riley entertained his family with stories of the African bush, Hendrik and Chad, the angry elephant, and the mysterious black rhino. His hat proved to be very helpful in tracking neighborhood pets as he returned to living the life of a nine year old...until the mail arrived with a new letter from Uncle Max.

Where will he go next?

FURTHER INFORMATION

Glossary

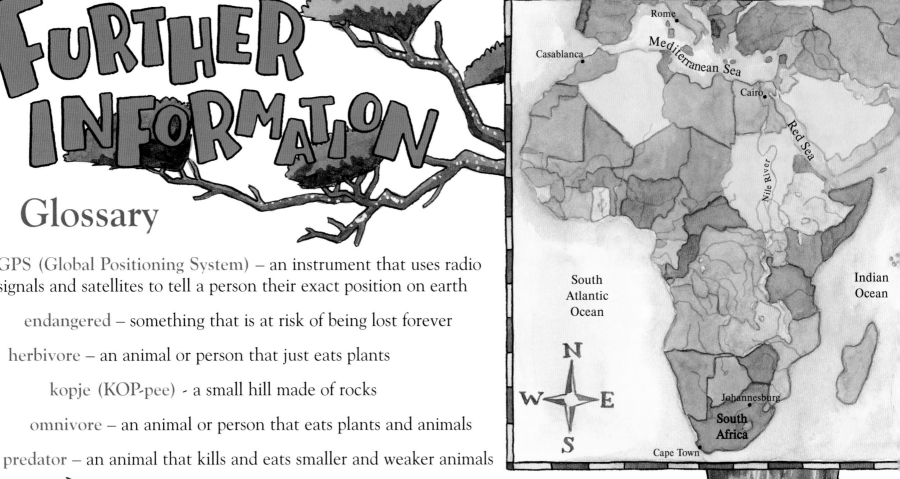

GPS (Global Positioning System) – an instrument that uses radio signals and satellites to tell a person their exact position on earth

endangered – something that is at risk of being lost forever

herbivore – an animal or person that just eats plants

kopje (KOP-pee) - a small hill made of rocks

omnivore – an animal or person that eats plants and animals

predator – an animal that kills and eats smaller and weaker animals

prey – a smaller or weaker animal that has to run quick or it will become a predator's meal

radiator – a device in a car usually filled with water that can overheat if empty

scavenger – animals that eat or steal other animals' prey

species – different kinds of plants and animals

survive – to continue to live

WHAT ARE THESE?

Hidden inside pages of each *Adventures of Riley* book are two compass drawings. Finding them will help you unlock Further Adventures (continuing storylines beyond the pages of the book) on Riley's website.

Visit Riley's World on-line at
www.adventuresofriley.com
and click on "Further Adventures" for more information.

PASSPORT INSTRUCTIONS

1. Have an adult help you to carefully remove the Passport from the book.

2. Fold it in half so that the **Adventure Sticker** circles are in the inside.

3. Write your Name, Birthday and Today's Date on the front.

4. Peel off the included sticker and place onto any open circle on the inside of the Passport to mark where you and Riley went. (There is a a different sticker for each book in the *Adventures of Riley* series!)

5. Visit www.adventuresofriley.com or fill out and mail in the enclosed card to register your Passport and become a member of **RILEY'S WORLD** – a fun, FREE and educational web site loaded with games and activities! (You will need a parent or guardian to help you with this.)

6. After you are registered, you will receive an Official Gold Membership Sticker for the front of your Passport *plus many other fun surprises!*

Come and see what is happening at Riley's World!

Become an Official Member of Riley's World and receive a gold membership sticker for your passport!

Membership is EASY and FREE!

Just go to:

www.adventuresofriley.com

to sign up for loads of fun and educational games, further adventures, and great savings!

Passport

to

RILEY'S WORLD

Official Gold Membership Sticker Goes Here

Name	Birthday	Date